Brian's Bird

WRITTEN BY **Patricia A. Davis**

ILLUSTRATED BY **Layne Johnson**

Albert Whitman & Company
Morton Grove, Illinois

Patricia A. Davis was a teacher of visually impaired children in the Baltimore County Public Schools from 1973 to 1997. She taught Braille and other special skills. Brian Johnson was her student from 1994 to 1997.

Layne Johnson was born and raised in Houston, Texas, and received a bachelor of fine arts degree from the University of Houston. He has artwork in corporate and private collections. This is his third book for children.

Library of Congress Cataloging-in-Publication Data

Davis, Patricia Anne.
Brian's bird / by Patricia A. Davis ; illustrated by Layne Johnson.
p. cm.
Summary: Eight-year-old Brian, who is blind, learns how to take care of
his new parakeet and comes to realize that his older brother,
while sometimes careless, is not so bad after all.
ISBN 0-8075-0881-0
[Parakeets Fiction. 2. Pets Fiction. 3. Brothers Fiction.
4. Blind Fiction. 5. Physically handicapped Fiction.] I. Johnson, Layne, ill. II. Title.
PZ7.D29743Br 2000   [Fic]—dc21   99-36094
CIP

The design is by Scott Piehl.

To Brian Lavon Johnson, an inspiration
to everyone. — P. A.D.

Thanks to Todd, Patrick, Ella, Nedra,
and Eric. And especially to my guiding light,
my love, my Sondra. — L. J.

QUICK FOOTSTEPS banged down the path behind Brian. "Beat you, Bri!" shouted his brother, Kevin, as he ran into the house.

Brian sighed. "Kevin always beats me," he said to himself. "Maybe when I get older . . ." But Brian doubted that it would make much difference. Kevin would be older, too.

Brian climbed the steps to the front door and reached for the knob. It wasn't there! He felt around for it and then realized that the door was standing open. The boys were supposed to shut the door behind them, but Kevin forgot half the time.

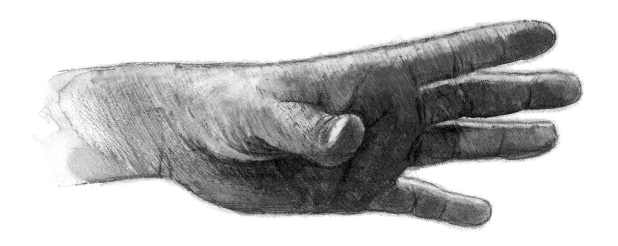

Brian went inside and closed the door. Then he stopped and listened.

He heard his family's voices in the kitchen.

Suddenly, everyone shouted, "Happy birthday, Brian!" Daddy, Momma, Kevin, and Grandma were all wishing him a happy birthday. He was eight years old today.

"Your presents are on the table," said Kevin.

Brian reached out. He expected to find a box covered in wrapping paper, but his fingers touched something made of hard, stiff wires. Surprised, Brian jumped back!

"It's OK," said Momma.

He reached out again and carefully felt the wire thing all over. It was square...no...rectangle-shaped, and round on top with a handle.

"A cage?" asked Brian.

"Yes, a cage," said Momma, "and there's a bird in it."

"A bird!" shouted Brian. "For me? What's it look like? What color is it?"

Brian couldn't see anything now, but long ago, when he was four or five, he had been able to see a little. He always asked what new things looked like. And he always wanted to know what color they were.

"He's about as tall as the salt shaker," said Momma. "He's green with a yellow head, and he's called a parakeet. You can teach him to talk."

"And he's tame," said Grandma. "I'll show you."

Brian heard a little click. Then he heard the bird's wings fluttering.

"He's on my finger, Brian," Grandma said. "Reach your hand in beside mine."

Brian slowly put his hand into the cage. The bird jumped off Grandma's finger and fluttered his wings. Brian pulled his hand out quickly.

"You and the bird are both a little afraid. You'll soon get to know each other," said Daddy.

"We'll try again later," said Grandma. "He needs to get used to his new home."

That night Brian and Grandma sat in the kitchen. "Now we'll get the bird out and let him sit on your finger," said Grandma. "Make sure the front door is closed, because if the bird gets out, he may never come back."

Brian went to check. "It's closed," he said.

Grandma showed Brian how to open the cage door. In a few seconds, she said, "The bird is on my finger. I'm bringing him out of the cage. Now stick your finger out."

Slowly, Brian stuck out his finger. Grandma moved his hand until his finger touched something soft and warm. Then two little feet stepped onto Brian's finger. They felt funny. Brian laughed.

"After the bird gets used to you, you'll be able to pet him," Grandma said. "What are you going to call him?"

"How about Scratchy?" said Brian. "Because that's the way he feels on my finger!"

"Momma said I could teach him to talk," said Brian. "How do I do that?"

"You have to say something to him over and over," said Grandma. "After a while, he'll learn to say it."

"Hello, Scratchy," said Brian. "Hello, Scratchy."

"Better say, 'Hello, *Brian*,'" said Grandma.

"Why should I say hello to myself?"

"Because the bird will repeat exactly what you say," Grandma told him.

Brian practiced with his bird every day. He put his hand in the cage and said, "Come on, Scratchy." Scratchy sat on his finger, and Brian pulled his hand out. Then Brian would say, "Hello, Brian. Hello, Brian." Scratchy would listen. Sometimes he chirped, but he never said a word.

When Scratchy flew around the room, Brian sat still and held up his hand. "Come on, Scratchy," he would say. Usually Scratchy would fly down and sit on Brian's finger.

Sometimes he flew right out of the room. Then Brian had to call Grandma. "Come and help me find Scratchy. I'm afraid if he's on the floor, I might step on him."

When Grandma found him, she would tell Brian where he was. Brian would reach up, hold out his finger, and say, "Come on, Scratchy."

By this time the bird was tired. He would fly down and land on Brian's finger. Then Brian would carefully put him in his cage.

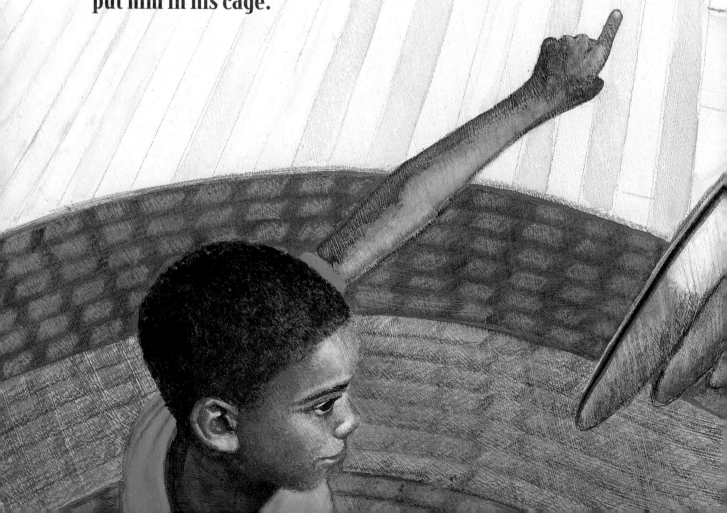

EXTENSION

One day when Brian came in after school, a strange voice said, "Hello, Brian."

"Who's that?" asked Brian.

The voice spoke again. "Hello, Brian," it repeated.

Was someone teasing him? Brian was about to call Grandma when he realized the voice came from the corner where the birdcage stood. "Was that you, Scratchy?" he asked.

"Hello, Brian." The voice came right out of the birdcage!

"Grandma! Kevin!" yelled Brian. "Come quick! Scratchy can talk!"

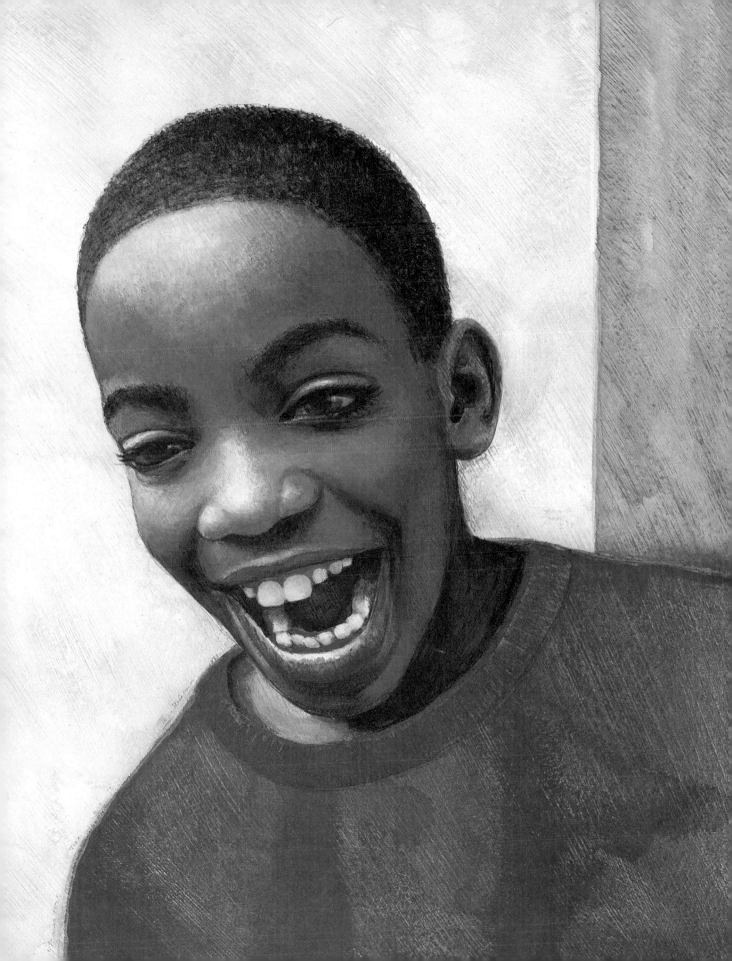

Grandma and Kevin came. They stood and listened, but Scratchy did not say a thing. "I don't believe it," said Kevin. "You're making it up." He left the room.

"I can't stand him," grumbled Brian.

"I know," said Grandma. "Big brothers can be a pain. Can you think of anything good about him?"

"Well," replied Brian, "sometimes he takes me for ice cream, and he never lets anyone pick on me."

"Sounds like he's not a half-bad brother," said Grandma.

That night after dinner, a strange voice said, "Hello, Brian."
Everyone stopped talking in surprise. "Who said that?" asked Daddy.

"Scratchy!" shouted Brian. "My bird can talk!"

Brian's bird learned to say a lot of things after that. He said, "Hello, Brian. I like you." He said, "Come on, Scratchy." He said, "See you later!"

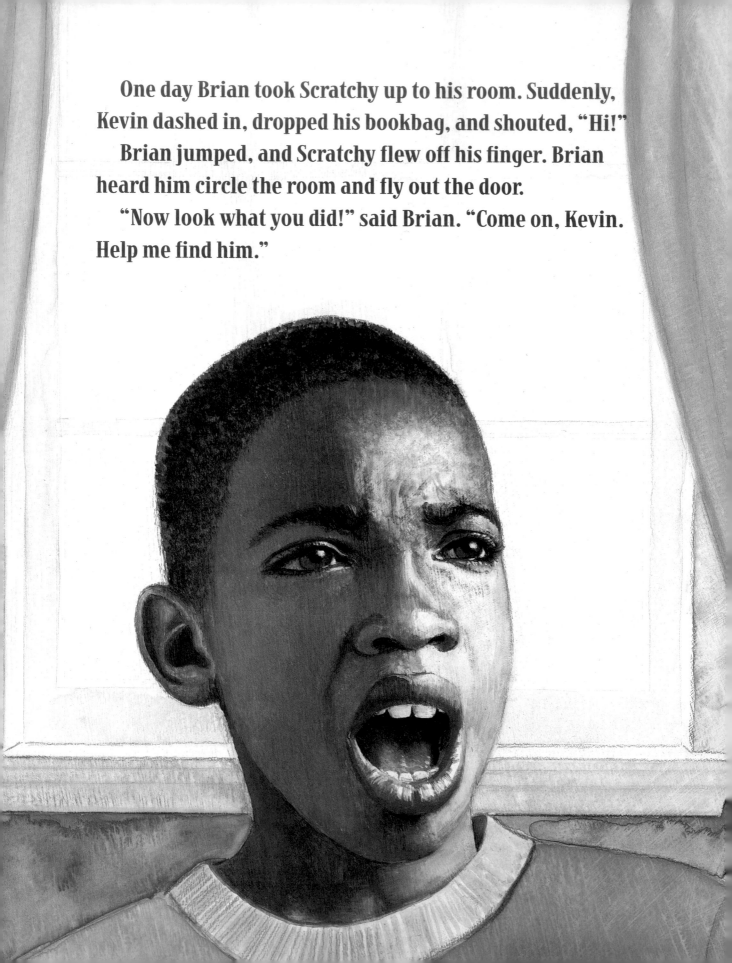

One day Brian took Scratchy up to his room. Suddenly, Kevin dashed in, dropped his bookbag, and shouted, "Hi!"

Brian jumped, and Scratchy flew off his finger. Brian heard him circle the room and fly out the door.

"Now look what you did!" said Brian. "Come on, Kevin. Help me find him."

The boys rushed into the living room. "I don't see him," said Kevin. "Uh-oh! The front door's open! He must have flown outside!"

"Oh, no! Kevin, you forgot to close the door! Now my bird is gone!" Brian was ready to cry.

"I see him, Brian! He's on the little tree at the side of the steps. I could just reach up and grab him."

"No!" said Brian. "He'll fly away. Tell me exactly where he is."

"Go outside; take two steps forward and one to the right; then hold up your finger."

Brian followed Kevin's directions. He held up his finger and said, "Come on, Scratchy."

Nothing happened.

Then Kevin's voice came softly from inside the house. "Take one more step forward, Brian. Then move a little closer to the tree, and hold up your hand as high as you can. You'll be as close as you can get then."

Brian took a step forward. He stood on his tiptoes and stretched his arm up as high as he could. "Come on, Scratchy," he whispered. He heard a flutter of wings, and two little feet landed on his finger.

Brian slowly stepped back inside. "Shut the door, Kevin," he said.

Brian put the bird into the cage and closed it.

"I'm sorry, Brian," Kevin said. "I really am. I'll be more careful next time."

Brian sighed. He knew Kevin would never be as careful as he was. Still, without Kevin's help, he might not have caught Scratchy. And after such a scare, Kevin just *might* be more careful.

"That's OK, Kev," he said. "You helped me catch him. You're only a half-bad brother."

Brian stuck out his hand, palm up. "Gimme five," he said.

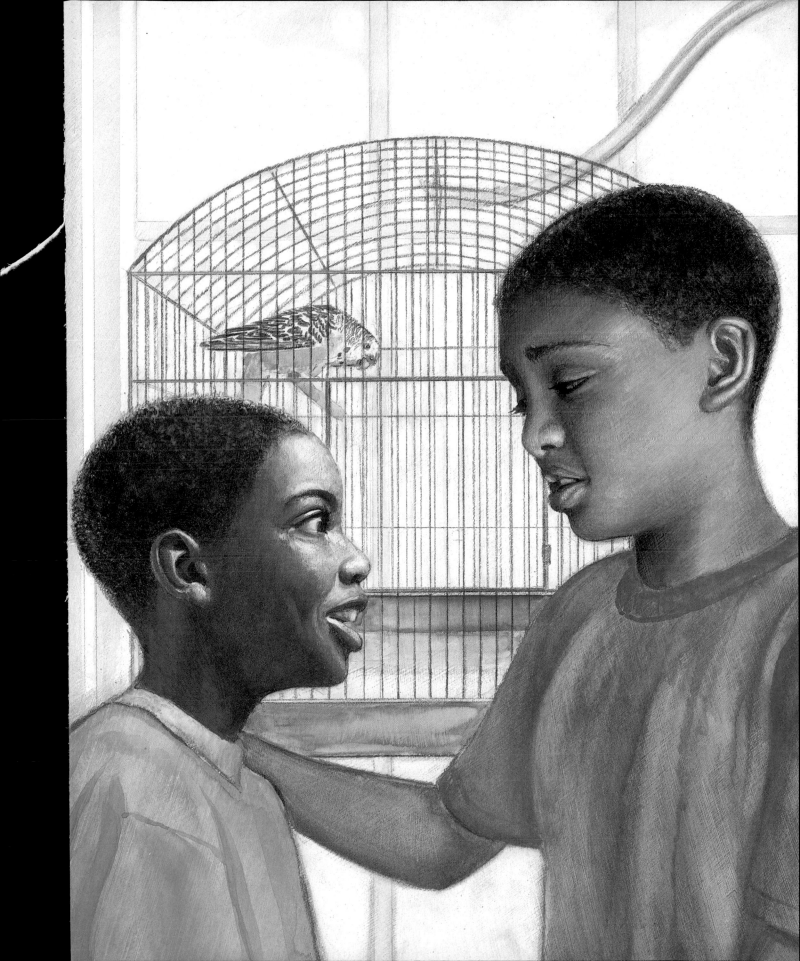

And Kevin did.

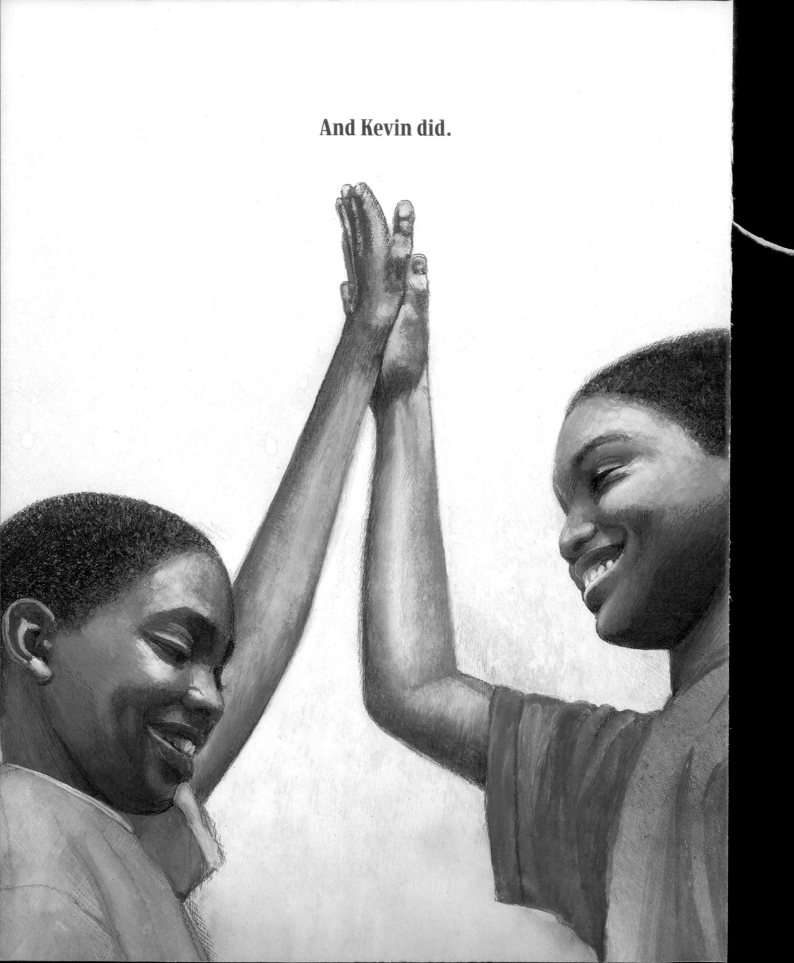